Petro Pete's Adventure

THE ROAD TO PETROVILLE

OKLAHOMA

OERB®

Written by
Landi Thompson &
Rachel Johnson

illustrated by
Cameron Eagle

First Edition 2008
"The Road to Petroville"
Written by Landi Thompson and Rachel Johnson
Copyright 2008 Oklahoma Energy Resources Board
www.oerb.com

Illustrations and graphic design copyright
Cameron Eagle, ink-ranch, inc. 2008
Printed in Oklahoma, USA

ISBN 978-0-615-19844-6

9 780615 198446   51500

Dedicated to Oklahoma's Oil and Natural Gas Producers and Royalty Owners.

Oklahoma Energy Resources Board

Created by the Oklahoma Legislature and energy industry leaders in 1993, the OERB is funded voluntarily by oil and natural gas producers and royalty owners through a one-tenth of 1 percent assessment on the sale of oil and natural gas. The OERB's purpose is to conduct environmental restoration of orphaned and abandoned well sites and to educate Oklahomans about the vitality, contributions and environmental responsibility of Oklahoma's oil and natural gas industry.

It was a cold winter night in Petroville, Oklahoma. Pappy Pete was tucking in his grandson, Petro Pete, but Pete did not want to go to sleep. "Okay, Pete, it's time for lights out," said Pappy.

"Wait!" exclaimed Pete. "Grand Pappy, will you tell me one more story... *please?*"

"Well ... alright," Pappy agreed. "What story do you want me to tell?"
Pete thought for a few minutes before asking, "Will you tell me the story
about how you and Grammy Petunia moved to Oklahoma?"

Smiling, Pappy said, "Well, when I moved to Oklahoma, I had no idea I would start out working as a worm!"

"A WORM?!?!" Pete exclaimed.

"Yes," Pappy chuckled. "A worm is just a term used by oilfield workers to describe someone new to the drilling industry."

"What made you want to be a worm?" Pete asked.

"It all started," Pappy began, "when I read in the local newspaper about the booming Oklahoma oil industry. There were big fortunes to be made. Your Grammy and I loaded up the wagon, moved to Oklahoma and never looked back."

"When we rolled into Petroville, we couldn't believe our eyes ... your Grammy Petunia was shocked by all of the people in Petroville."

"We could see why it was called a boomtown. I knew I had to find a job very quickly, or they all would be taken."

"We headed straight for the General Store to see if there were any job openings around town. When we walked in, the storeowner said, 'Howdy, y'all. Are ya new to the area? I don't recall seein' ya around these parts. I suppose yer lookin' fer work in the oil patch?'

"I asked him how he knew just by looking at me. He told me there were people coming in the store daily looking for work. They came by train, wagon, on horseback and on foot. Luckily, there were plenty of jobs available in the oil patch."

"Did you find a job, Pappy?" Pete asked.
"I sure did, Pete. I started work the very next day. In fact, your Grammy
had to find us a place to live all on her own!" Pappy explained.

"Not many of the oilfield workers had family around to cook them dinner," Pappy continued. "They gladly paid your Grammy 50 cents for one of her famous meals. For $5 a week, we gave workers a place to sleep and eat. There were so many people, even the barn was full! One fella even paid us to sleep on our roof!"

"Five dollars doesn't sound like much money to me," Pete replied. "My allowance is $5 a week!"

Laughing, Pappy said, "Well back then it was quite a lot of money. We only made $10 a day."

"Why did everyone sleep at your house?" Pete questioned.
"Didn't they have their own homes?"

Pappy replied, "They did have homes, but they were many miles away.
Not everyone had cars in those days."

"The men were too tired at the end of the day to walk or ride their ~~horses that far~~ most worked 12- to 18-hour days. All they wanted was a hot meal and a place to sleep. Working in the oil patch is hard work."

"I remember my first day like it was yesterday," Pappy recalled. "I showed up at the Petroville oil field just as Wildcatter Wally was explaining where we were going to drill. He held out his hand to show us a shiny wet rock with a peculiar smell ... the smell of oil! He told us there was no guarantee, but he thought there was oil under our feet."

"The first thing to be done was to build a wooden derrick so we could drill into the ground for the oil trapped in the rocks below."

"Once the construction crew was finished building the derrick, the drilling crew got to work," Pappy explained.

"Toolpusher Tommy was my boss. He oversaw the drilling crew.
He was on call at all times in case any of us needed him. He was the most
experienced man on our crew. At the drilling site, Tommy lived in a
shotgun house, a very small, one- or two-room house with doors at each
end. If the front and back doors were open, you could see right through it."

"Driller Dalton kept a close eye on the derrick hands and roughnecks to make sure the drilling went smoothly. When Toolpusher Tommy was trying to get a few hours of sleep, the crew relied on Driller Dalton for instruction."

"Derrickhand Dan was responsible for running drill pipe into the hole from the derrick. One length of drill pipe, called a joint, was 60 to 90 feet long. We put drill pipe into the hole to keep it from collapsing. By connecting these joints together, we could drill a well 2,000 feet deep, which isn't very deep considering today's wells can be more than 30,000 feet deep!"

"Roughneck Ralph and I handled the lower end of the drill pipe while Derrickhand Dan lowered the pipe from above. We used big wrenches called tongs to tighten the joints together. We also had to keep the rig clean and help repair it when things were broken."

"It sounds like a lot of work, Pappy," Pete said.

"It was hard work," Pappy replied, "but we had a great time. We never dreamed the work we were doing would play such an important role in the success of Oklahoma. That's why it is so important for you to learn about the oil and natural gas industry."

"Pappy, will you come to school and tell your stories to my class?" Pete asked.

Pappy smiled and said, "Why sure, Pete, but we can talk about that in the morning. It's past your bedtime."

"Goodnight, Pappy. I love you."

"Love you, too, Pete. Sweet dreams."

THE END

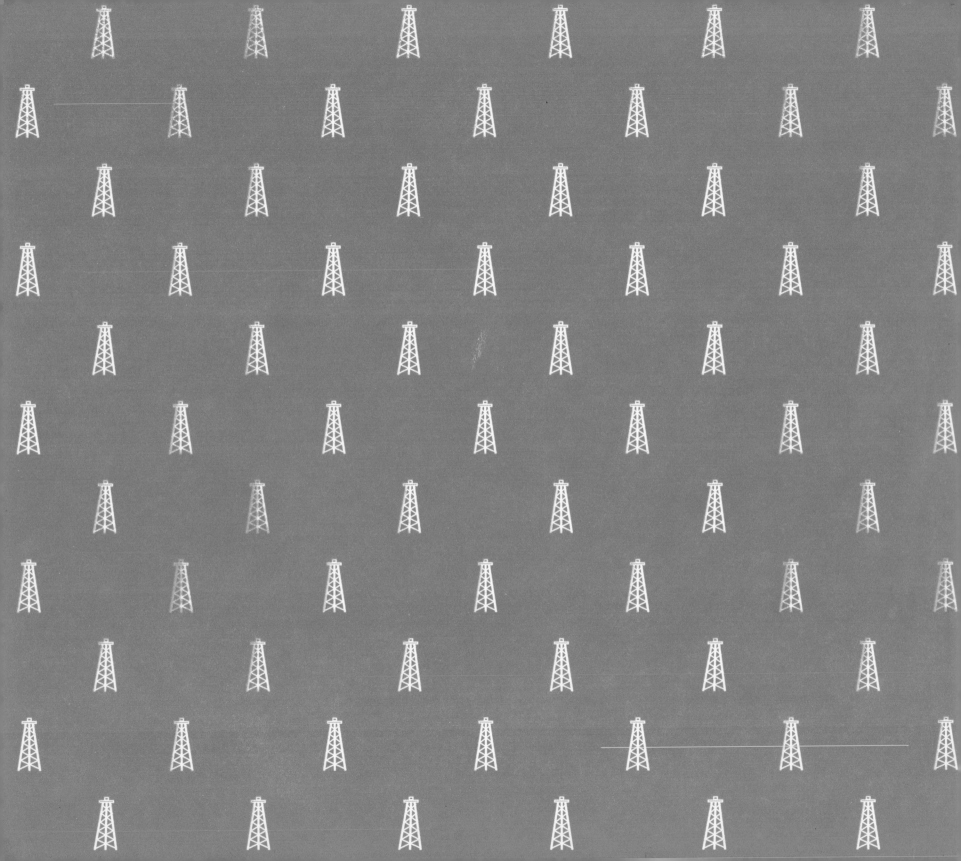